# MUSEUM MYSTERIES

Museum Mysteries is published by Stone Arch Books
A Capstone Imprint
1710 Roe Crest Drive
North Mankato, MN 56003
www.mycapstonepub.com

Library of Congress Cataloging-in-Publication Data is available on the Library of Congress website.

ISBN 978-1-4965-2518-5 (hardcover) — ISBN 978-1-4965-2522-2 (paperback) — ISBN 978-1-4965-2526-0 (eBook PDF) — 978-1-4965-3330-2 (reflowable epub)

Summary: Clementine Wim spots a famous painting being carried away from the Capitol City Art Museum. But when she arrives at the museum, the painting is hanging right where it should be. It's up to Clementine to convince her friends that what she saw was real and determine fact from forgery before it's too late.

Designer: K. Carlson
Editor: A. Deering
Production Specialist: K. McColley

Photo Credits: Shutterstock (vector images, backgrounds, paper textures)

Printed and bound in China.
007734

# The Case of the
# COUNTERFEIT PAINTING

By Steve Brezenoff
Illustrated by Lisa K. Weber

STONE ARCH BOOKS
a capstone imprint

# Ralph Goings

- Ralph Goings is an American painter who was born in California in 1928, during the height of the Great Depression.

- Goings is recognized as one of the founders of the Photorealism movement, which began in the late 1960s.

- Goings is best known for his highly detailed, realistic paintings of everyday items such as tabletops, supermarkets, hamburger stands, pickup trucks, and later, New York diners.

- Many of Goings's most famous paintings hang in galleries, including the Museum of Modern Art, the Whitney, and the Guggenheim in New York and the Museum of Contemporary Art in Chicago, Illinois.

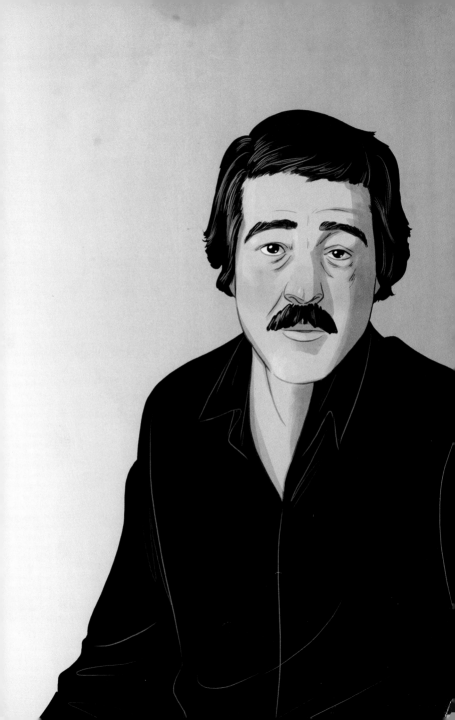

Amal Farah

Raining Sam

Wilson Kipper

Clementine Wim

# Capitol City Sleuths

### Amal Farah
Age: 11
Favorite Museum: Air and Space Museum
Interests: astronomy, space travel, and
building models of spaceships

### Raining Sam
Age: 12
Favorite Museum: American History Museum
Interests: Ojibwe history, culture, and
traditions, American history — good and bad

### Clementine Wim
Age: 13
Favorite Museum: Art Museum
Interests: painting, sculpting with clay, and
anything colorful

### Wilson Kipper
Age: 10
Favorite Museum: Natural History Museum
Interests: dinosaurs (especially pterosaurs
and herbivores) and building dinosaur models

# TABLE OF

# CONTENTS

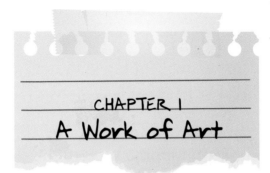

## CHAPTER 1
## A Work of Art

Clementine Wim was alone.

Though she loved her friends, she was also the sort of person who enjoyed being alone every so often, mainly because that was the best time for art. And there was nothing Clementine enjoyed more than working on her art.

This particular Saturday morning, Clementine's hands were caked in reddish clay, and her hair — which she'd meant to tie back in a bun — kept falling over her eyes. There was probably clay in her hair, too, but she had no time to worry about that. Instead, she kept blowing her hair off her face as her hands went to work on the spinning wet clay in front of her. Her right foot kept hopping to keep the clay spinning on the potter's wheel.

The potter's wheel was fairly new to her — Dad had found a cheap one at a garage sale the previous weekend and had fixed it up for Clementine to keep in the shed, her makeshift studio. After several failures before breakfast, she finally seemed to be getting the hang of it.

"This one looks pretty good," Clementine muttered to herself as the hourglass-shaped vase began to form in front of her.

Just then, the phone on the bench next to her began to chirp and vibrate. She glanced down at its glowing screen.

*Wilson calling . . . Wilson calling . . . Wilson calling . . .*

Clementine sighed. Wilson Kipper — her best friend. As much as she wanted to keep working, she couldn't just ignore it. So, with her foot still pumping on the wheel's pedal, she scooped up the phone. Trying her best to keep the phone free of wet clay, she nestled it between her shoulder and ear.

"Hello?" Clementine answered.

"Where *are* you?" Wilson said on the other end. There were lots of excited, joyful voices, too, as if Wilson were at a party or something.

"Where am I?" Clementine said. "Where are *you*?"

"The Big Lawn!" Wilson said. He waited a beat. "You forgot, didn't you?"

"Oh, no," Clementine said. She looked down at the spinning vase as it began to wobble. "What did I forget?"

"The Natural History Museum party on the Lawn," he said. "The Dino Festival!"

Clementine stopped pedaling. Wilson's mom worked at the Natural History Museum, and Clementine had planned to meet Wilson and their friends Raining Sam and Amal Farrah there first thing this morning for the big event.

"I'm sorry," she said. "I did forget. But I'll leave right now. I'll be there so fast you won't believe it. Bye!"

Clementine grabbed her phone to hang up, but as soon as she did, she remembered her hands were covered in clay. She squealed and tossed the phone sky high. It knocked into the shed's ceiling and dropped back down — right into the unfinished vase. The top of the vase collapsed on itself, sealing the phone in the wet clay.

"Ah!" Clementine screamed, but it was hopeless. The reddish mass held her phone like some kind of space-age super putty. It was stuck, and she had no time to try to fish it out.

Wiping her hands on a towel, Clementine grabbed her helmet and took off on her bike, heading for the Big Lawn.

## CHAPTER 2
## Just a Glimpse

The Big Lawn — its official name — was an expanse of manicured green, crisscrossed with sidewalks and low bushes. It sat at the top of the hill between the four Capitol City museums. While it was usually quiet and calm — sometimes used by museum visitors to get from one museum to another — today the Big Lawn was being utterly trampled.

Clementine chained her bike to the rack behind the Art Museum, where her mother,

Dr. Abigail Wim, worked, and moved toward the crowd. Almost immediately, she was sucked into the mass of people.

"Oh, boy," Clementine muttered. "There's no way I'll find them!" Every kid in Capitol City must have been there, along with his or her entire family.

The Dino Festival was a special event for kids of all ages, but Clementine hadn't realized people took that expression so literally. She'd expected to see kids around her age and her friends' ages, but there were babies and grandparents here, toddlers and moms and dads.

"Chaos!" Clementine exclaimed, taking her head in her hands. Still, she pushed on through the crowd, making her way through the maze of tents and kiosks and animatronic dinosaurs that the museum had moved outside from the courtyard of the Natural History Museum.

After shoving and getting shoved, delivering dozens of *excuse me's* and *beg your pardon's*, Clementine found herself on the far side of the Lawn, still without having found her friends.

"Clementine?" a voice called, not far off. "What are you doing here all alone?"

Clementine turned and found the speaker right away — Dr. Carolyn Kipper, Wilson's mom and one of the Natural History Museum's paleontologists.

"I am quite alone," Clementine said. "Unfortunately. I've been searching and searching for your son — and Raining and Amal. Have you seen them?"

Dr. Kipper shook her head. "Not in the last hour or so," she said, planting her fists on her hips and twisting her face in thought. "They were at the Fossil Dig tent, but I can't imagine they'd still be there."

"Okay," Clementine said. "Thanks anyway. If you see them, will you tell them I'm looking for them?"

"Of course," Dr. Kipper said. "I'd better get back to my post."

"Oh, what exhibit are you at today?" Clementine asked.

Dr. Kipper clasped her hands in joy. "The Dino Family Tree!" she said. "It shows how a Tyrannosaurus rex is more closely related to a chickadee than to a Stegosaurus!"

Clementine laughed. "And people say I'm weird!" she said. "See you, Dr. Kipper."

She turned away and spent several minutes wandering the edges of the festival. She'd nearly given up hope when she stumbled into a man. "Oh, excuse me."

"Why don't you watch where you're going?" the man snapped. He was a bit taller than Clementine and had a big black beard. On his head he wore a black baseball cap, and in his arms he held the back end of a huge, covered rectangle.

"Oh, be nice," the woman holding the front end of the rectangle admonished him. "Can't you see the poor girl is lost?"

"Oh, I'm not lost," said Clementine. "But my friends are. That is, I can't find them. Have you seen them?"

"Well, I don't know," the woman said with a little laugh. "Who are they?"

Clementine described her three best friends and then added her phone number to the other woman's cell phone. Her hands were full, so Clementine made sure to save it in the list of contacts. "If you see them, please call me," she said.

"I sure will," the woman said, taking her phone back and jamming it into her back pocket. She gave Clementine a big grin. "We'd better be moving on now."

"Finally!" the man snapped.

They started shuffling off, carrying that big rectangle between them, when Clementine felt a tug under her foot. She'd somehow stepped on the white sheet that was covering their load.

"Oh, whoops!" Clementine said, hopping off. A bit of the sheet slipped off the bottom

of the rectangle, though, exposing a small patch of blue and white. "What is that?" she asked.

"None of your business!" the man snapped, quickly covering the exposed corner. "Just watch your step before you do some *real* damage."

"I'm sorry," Clementine said with a frown. She really was sorry, but she was still thinking about that patch of blue and white.

Suddenly, Clementine knew exactly what it was. She'd seen those blue and white squares hundreds of times — maybe more than hundreds. It was the corner of a painting of three men sitting at an old-fashioned lunch counter. Her mom had the poster hanging in their kitchen because it was going to be the main feature of her upcoming exhibit on Photorealism at the Capitol City Art Museum.

The original painting was worth millions. And the two people she'd just met should *not* have been carrying it around. In fact, it was supposed to be hanging in her mom's art museum *right now.*

## CHAPTER 3
### Stolen?

Clementine ran madly around the Dino Festival. She had to find the people with the painting again — and she had to find her friends. If anyone could help her with this new case — *a stolen painting!* — it was her three best friends.

But as much as Clementine searched, the man and the woman and their rectangle were gone. Before long, the Dino Festival started winding down. People left to get lunch and continue on with the day, and soon the crowd was sparse. But Clementine's friends were still nowhere to be seen.

"Clementine Wim!" shouted a familiar voice. "Are you still here?"

"Hi, Dr. Kipper," Clementine said. Wilson's mom was carrying a big crate overflowing with model dinosaur bones. They were piled so high, she had to peek around the side to look at Clementine. "Yup, I'm still here. I haven't found Wilson and the others yet. But I did see something weird —"

"I can't really chat, dear," Dr. Kipper said. "I have to get this stuff back to the stock room at the museum. But I think your friends went over to the Art Museum to find you."

"Thanks, Dr. Kipper!" Clementine said, waving goodbye. She didn't even bother getting her bike. She just sprinted down the grass and around to the front of the Art Museum. She waved and smiled at the security guards and ticket-takers. They all knew her, of course, and they all smiled and waved back.

Clementine ran toward the back of the museum, where her mother's office was located, but she didn't get far. As she sped past the room for the new special exhibit on Photorealism, she spotted something out of the corner of her eye — white and ice-blue squares.

"What?" Clementine exclaimed, skidding to a halt, just as Wilson, Amal, and Raining came out of the Photorealism exhibit.

"Clementine, finally!" Wilson said. "Where have you *been*?"

"We've been calling you and calling you!" Amal said, holding up her phone as if to prove it.

But Clementine ignored her friends and walked right past them into the Photorealism exhibit.

"Clementine!" her mother said. Dr. Wim stood in the middle of the exhibit. It had been her pet project for months, and Clementine could see how proud she was just by looking at her.

But for now, Clementine ignored her mom, too. She marched right up to the painting in the center of the far wall, which had caught her eye as she'd run by — three men on stools with their backs to the viewer, seated at an old-fashioned lunch counter tiled in ice-blue and white tiles.

"There it is," Dr. Wim said as she put an arm around her daughter's shoulders. *"Tiled Lunch Counter*, by Ralph Goings. It's just overwhelming in person, isn't it? It dwarfs the poster we have at home — Clementine, what's wrong?"

Clementine stood at the velvet rope in front of the painting and stared at the canvas. "I don't understand," she said, almost under her breath. "I was so sure."

"So sure of what, dear?" Dr. Wim said. She gave Clementine a quizzical look.

"Um . . . ," Clementine said. She pulled away from her mother. "Nothing. Never mind."

She paced toward the benches in the center of the gallery. She'd been certain — those two people on the Big Lawn had been carrying that painting. She was sure of it. She'd *seen* it. Well, she'd seen a little bit of it, at least. But the little bit she'd seen had definitely been part of *that* painting.

"What's up, Clementine?" Wilson said as he sat down next to her. "You look like you saw a ghost."

"Nothing," Clementine said, shaking her head and forcing a smile. There was no reason to worry her friends. "Sorry I was late today. I looked all over for you guys, but it was a madhouse. I couldn't find you anywhere."

Wilson started to reply, but Clementine tuned him out, still focused on the painting. She could have been wrong, really. After all, she wasn't the expert her mother was, and clearly the painting wasn't missing.

*If I could just get a closer look*, Clementine thought, *maybe I'll see something — something wrong.*

She stood up and walked back to the Goings painting.

"Clementine?" Wilson called after her. "What are you doing?"

"Why is she being so weird?" Amal asked.

"Beats me," Raining said, shrugging his shoulders. Clementine's odd behavior wasn't exactly a new phenomenon.

Clementine stepped up to the velvet rope, right next to her mother, and stared hard at the corner of the painting, where the blue and white tiles seemed to shine. That was the magic of Photorealism.

"Darling, I have to get to my office," Dr. Wim said. "I'll see you at home later, okay?"

"Okay," Clementine said, barely hearing her mom and hardly noticing the kiss on the cheek she left her with. She was too intent on getting a closer look at the painting.

"If I could just get a closer look," Clementine whispered to herself, leaning over the velvet rope. She leaned so far, in fact, that the rope pulled on the posts holding it up, knocking them down with a tremendous *clang!*

"Watch what you're doing!" bellowed the security guard standing nearby. He was a big man with a wide, grumpy-looking face. Clementine didn't remember seeing him before at the museum, but he looked familiar somehow, just the same. "Back up from the painting please!"

"I'm sorry," Clementine said. She struggled to lift the posts. Raining ran over to help her, but the security guard shooed them both away. "I didn't mean to. I just wanted to get a closer look."

"Oh, I suppose you think you're entitled to a closer look than every other guest at the museum, huh?" the security guard said as he fixed the velvet rope.

"No!" Clementine protested. "It's just that —" She hesitated. She couldn't say out loud that she'd seen the very same painting on the Lawn a couple of hours ago. She'd sound crazy. "I wanted to see the brushstrokes. I'm a-an artist."

"Ooh," the security guard said, rolling his eyes mockingly. His voice was thick with sarcasm. "An artist. Well, then. Why don't I arrange a special tour for you?"

"Really?" Clementine said.

"No, not really!" the guard snapped. "Now back off!"

Clementine stood there for a moment with her mouth hanging open, but she knew if she continued to argue, she'd be in tears. So she turned her back on the guard, her friends, and *Tiled Lunch Counter* and ran from the gallery.

## CHAPTER 5
## Nothing to Solve

Clementine fully intended to forget
all about what had happened earlier
that day. She'd found her friends at the
museum, and more importantly, she'd
found the painting at the museum. If
there had been any mystery, it was over,
solved by destiny.

But after dinner, as she paced the floor of her little room in the funny half story at the top of her house, she couldn't get it out of her mind. The image of ice-blue and white tiles appeared before her like ghosts. She was sure she'd seen them. She was sure those two people at the Dino Festival had been carrying *Tiled Lunch Counter*.

"Or," she muttered to the empty room, "they were carrying a giant photograph of blue and white tiles. Which is possible. I guess."

Clementine fell backward onto her bed. "I have to tell Mom," she finally told herself, staring at the mural on her ceiling. She'd painted it herself, and it wasn't her best, but sometimes the swirling blues and specks of white looked enough like Vincent van Gogh's *Starry Night* that she didn't mind it too much.

With a sigh, Clementine hopped up and headed downstairs. She found her mother at the kitchen table. There were papers and photos spread out all over.

"What are you doing?" Clementine asked as she sat down. The poster of *Tiled Lunch Counter* still hung over the table. It seemed so small now that she'd seen the real thing at the museum.

Mom didn't look up from her work. "Planning our next special exhibit," she said. "Or trying to, anyway."

Clementine picked up a photo from the table to take a better look. It was a painting of a dog — the kind people sometimes called wiener dogs — on a leash. But the dog in the image seemed to have a hundred blurry feet, and so did the person walking it.

"What's this?" Clementine asked.

Mom looked over the top of her reading glasses for a moment. "That is . . . ," she said, "*Dynamism of a Dog on a Leash*, an example of the Italian Futurism movement. Do you like it?"

Clementine shrugged. "I guess."

"Something on your mind?" Mom asked. She could always tell when Clementine was distraught.

"Kind of," Clementine said, leaning forward on her elbows and propping her chin on her fists. "Something weird happened to me today."

"Are you hurt?" Mom asked, quickly taking off her reading glasses and looking concerned.

"No," Clementine said, shaking her head. "Nothing like that."

"Good," Mom said, sounding relieved. "So what happened?"

"I saw *Tiled Lunch Counter* today," Clementine said.

Mom looked perplexed. "So did I," she replied. "It's on exhibit at the museum. Not to mention it's hanging over our heads right now."

"The poster, yes," Clementine said. She looked up at the poster again, and at the blue and white tiles in the bottom-right corner. "But I mean I saw it at the Dino Festival."

"You went to the Dino Festival?" Mom asked. She tilted her head slightly in confusion. "Isn't that for little kids?"

"I was supposed to meet Wilson and my other friends there," Clementine explained.

Mom nodded in understanding. "Ah," she said. "Anyway, what do you mean? How could you have seen the painting there?"

"Well, that's why it's *weird*," Clementine said.

Taking a deep breath, she quickly told her mom about what she'd seen earlier — all about the woman and the man with the big beard and the giant rectangle and the corner of blue and white tiles.

"That's why I was so shocked when I got to the Art Museum," Clementine finished. "I figured it had been stolen."

"That is strange," her mom said. "But it certainly wasn't stolen. You saw it yourself. Do you know what I think?"

"What?" Clementine asked.

"I think that in your mind," Mom said, "you *did* see it. You and I have been staring at this poster for weeks. I see those blue and white tiles when I close my eyes at night to go to sleep. I see it everywhere I look!"

"You mean, it's on my mind even if I don't know it," Clementine said, "just because I see the poster so much?"

"Exactly," Mom said, nodding. "Maybe whatever those people were carrying *did* have some blue and white in it — maybe even a shade of blue similar to the one Goings used in his painting. That could have made your eyes and mind *think* you were seeing the painting."

Clementine leaned back in her chair and stared at the poster. "You really think so?" she said.

"I really do," Mom replied. She put her reading glasses back on and snatched *Dynamism of a Dog on a Leash* back from Clementine.

"I guess you're right," Clementine said. "Thanks, Mom."

"Anytime, sweetie," Mom said, turning back to her work.

Clementine headed back up to her room. *Mom is probably right*, she thought.

*After all, the painting was right there in the museum. It can't have been on the Lawn, too — unless one of them is a copy.*

## CHAPTER 6
## One-Track Mind

The next morning, Clementine got an early start out in the shed. Her vase — or what used to be a vase — had dried with her phone inside it. She almost felt bad about it. After all, the phone would come in handy. But the vase — sagged and flopped around her cell phone — had taken on such a fantastic abstract shape that Clementine couldn't bring herself to destroy it just for some silly phone.

Mom would understand — she hoped.

Instead, she decided to paint it. It didn't take her long to choose just the right color, and when Mom walked into the shed, Clementine was nearly done with the first coat of paint.

"Still thinking about *Tiled Lunch Counter*, huh?" Mom said.

"What do you mean?" Clementine asked, freezing mid-stroke. She looked at the vase, then up at Mom.

"Clementine, look at your sculpture," Mom said, putting a hand on her daughter's shoulder.

Clementine looked again. It was warped and twisted and nearly covered in paint the same color as the reflecting pool in the Art Museum courtyard on a calm, cloudless day. The same color as the blue tiles that made up the lunch counter in Goings's famous painting.

"Oh," Clementine said, and her shoulders sagged. "I see what you mean."

Mom patted her back. "Why don't you go up to the Big Lawn?" she said. "Hang out with your friends. They're at the Dino Festival again."

"How do you know?" Clementine asked.

"They called the house," Mom said. "They said they'd been calling your cell phone, but you haven't answered."

"Oh, right," Clementine said. "I thought I heard it ringing."

"Why didn't you answer?"

Clementine pointed at the blue sculpture.

"It's in there?" Mom said, raising her eyebrows.

Clementine nodded. "I couldn't bring myself to smash it and get the phone out."

Mom rolled her eyes. "Get going."

This time, when Clementine got to the festival, she found her friends right away. They made it easy on her — when she pulled up to the bike rack, they were waiting for her.

"Why haven't you answered your phone all morning?" Amal demanded. She crossed her arms.

"Or last night!" Wilson added.

"It fell into some clay," Clementine said.

"And it's broken?" Raining asked.

"No," Clementine said.

"Lost?" Wilson guessed.

"No," Clementine said, shaking her head. "It's still in the clay."

"Why don't you take it out?" Amal said, sounding angry.

"I can't just take it out," Clementine protested. "It's art now."

Her friends all looked at her like she was nuts. Sometimes they just didn't get it.

"Well, come on," Wilson said, taking her hand. "I want to show you all the cool stuff you missed yesterday."

Clementine followed Wilson into the Dino Festival, but no matter how many exhibits and activities they checked out, Clementine could hardly fake being interested.

"Guys," she finally said as she stopped somewhere between the Fake Fossil Find and the Pteradon Ptake-Off Ptent. "Can we go to the Art Museum? I want to look at the new exhibit."

"Didn't we look at that yesterday?" Amal said. "Like, before you got there, and then again after you ran off?"

Clementine looked at her shoes, which were splattered with ice-blue paint, and said nothing.

"Come on," Wilson said, stepping between Amal and Clementine. He took Clementine's hand again. "We can go to the Art Museum. It's fine."

"Why?" Amal said, sounding irritated and a little hurt. "Why should we? She hasn't exactly been a super friend lately."

"I'm sorry," Clementine said. "I — I can't really explain."

"Can you try to?" Wilson said.

"Let's go to the museum," Clementine said. "I'll explain there. I promise."

## CHAPTER 7
## Seeing Things?

Clementine almost gave up the moment she stepped foot into the special exhibit gallery. The same security guard from the day before — probably the meanest one Clementine had ever met — stood in front of *Tiled Lunch Counter*. He had his arms crossed and his chin down. His mouth was set in a straight, frightening line across his stony face.

Clementine hopped back out and peeked around the doorway. "He looks so familiar," she said.

"Who?" Wilson asked, looking and sounding confused.

"The security guard," Clementine said.

"Well, he works here," Amal said as she passed by Clementine and walked into the gallery. "Obviously you've seen him before. You practically live here."

Raining followed after Amal and went right into the special exhibit gallery. Wilson grabbed Clementine's wrist. "Come on," he said. "He's not going to bite."

Clementine took a deep breath and followed her friends inside. While the three of them wandered around the Photorealism exhibit, Clementine inched her way — as subtly as she could — toward *Tiled Lunch Counter*. When she reached the velvet rope, the security guard grunted.

Clementine huffed. "I swear," she said, "this rope is even farther back than it was yesterday."

"Maybe if we didn't have troublemakers like you hanging around," the guard snarled at her, "we wouldn't even need the rope. Ever think of that?"

"I can hardly see the painting from here!" Clementine said, stomping one foot.

"Then get glasses!" the guard snapped.

Clementine huffed again and retreated from the painting. Without getting closer, she'd never be able to tell if this painting was the real deal — or a very good copy.

She joined Wilson in front of a different painting in the exhibit. It seemed like the velvet rope in front of that painting was positioned much closer. Clementine squinted at the painting in front of them. It featured several bottles of makeup on a mirrored table with a silver cup in its center.

"Audrey Flack's *Chanel*," Clementine said. She glanced at the security guard. "I bet I could reach out and touch it."

"Don't," Wilson warned.

"I won't," Clementine said. "I mean, I wouldn't. But why is the rope so far back from the one painting in here I want a close look at?"

Wilson sighed. "Clem," he said, "why are you so obsessed with that painting? What is going on?"

Clementine felt her face get hot. "What do you mean?" she said.

"Come on, Clem," Wilson said, and he turned to face her. "You've been weird all morning. Not to mention yesterday when you ignored us at the museum and then ran out."

Clementine kept her eyes on *Chanel.* "Fine," she said. "I'll tell you, but you have to promise not to laugh."

"Of course I won't laugh," Wilson said. He was her best friend, after all.

With a sigh, Clementine told him the whole story, from the giant rectangle she'd seen on the Big Lawn, to the poster hanging in the kitchen, to her mom's theory about seeing things, right up to that point.

"And now this big gorilla of a security guard won't let me get close enough," Clementine finished.

"I'm still confused," Wilson said. "Why do you need to see it up close? The painting is there, isn't it? Even if you did see it on the Big Lawn, it's hanging where it's supposed to be now. And even if that's super weird, we know it wasn't stolen. If anything it was borrowed."

"Or," Clementine said, "the one I saw was the real one, and *this* one is a copy."

Wilson nodded. "Okay, I see what you mean," he admitted. "Then what do we need to do?"

"Help me get a closer look," Clementine said.

Wilson looked at the guard, then at Clementine, then at the guard again. "I don't know how," he said. "I mean, we'll need Amal and Raining, for sure, right?"

Clementine looked at Amal and Raining, both of whom were standing clear across the gallery. They'd both been blowing pretty cold and hot to her this morning, and she couldn't blame them. She'd been absent, weird, and grouchy for two days.

"I'll talk to them for you," Wilson said, and he started to head over there.

But Clementine grabbed his hand. "No," she said. "I can do it."

So with her chin up, Clementine strode across the gallery, banged her shin on the bench in the middle, snapped, "Gosh darnit," and dropped to the bench to hold her ankle.

Amal and Raining hurried to the bench. "Are you okay?" Amal said.

"What happened?" Raining said.

"Guys, I'm sorry," Clementine said. "I know I've been super weird."

"It's okay," they both said, sitting on either side of her.

"I'm going to explain," Clementine said. She lifted her chin toward *Tiled Lunch Counter*. "See that painting over there?"

Amal and Raining nodded.

"Well," Clementine said, "it all started at the Big Lawn yesterday when I couldn't find you three. . . ."

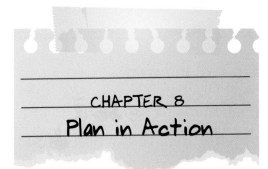

## CHAPTER 8
## Plan in Action

"Is everyone ready?" Amal asked a few minutes later.

As soon as Clementine had explained what was going on, Amal had come up with a plan. She was good at coming up with complicated plans, usually so they could get someplace they — strictly speaking — weren't supposed to go.

Sometimes it was an office. Sometimes it was a room full of security cameras. Once it had been a chartered tour bus.

Often it didn't work.

But Clementine's grouchy, distracted mood meant they really had to try.

"We're ready," Wilson said.

Raining nodded.

Clementine chewed her lip, tucked her hair behind her ear, and nodded. "I'm ready," she said. "Oh, I hope this works."

"It'll be fine," Amal said, getting up from the bench just outside the special exhibit. "Trust me."

Then she ran into the gallery, screaming, "Bees! Bees! So many bees!"

The other three waited outside and peeked around the doorway. "She's nuts," Raining said.

Wilson and Clementine nodded gravely.

The security guard next to *Tiled Lunch Counter* immediately snapped to attention as Amal tore through the gallery. She was shaking her T-shirt and shouting, "Bees! Bees! Thousands of *killer bees*!" over and over.

"Hey, what is this?" the guard said, and he stooped under the velvet rope and grabbed Amal by the elbow as she ran past. "What's going on?"

"Bees!" Amal shrieked in his face. She jumped up and down, slapping her shirt and shorts and hijab frantically.

"I don't see any bees," the guard said. Meanwhile, the other guests in the gallery had all turned to watch.

"This is your chance," Raining said to Clementine. "Go."

Clementine couldn't afford to wait. She hurried into the gallery. Amal saw her and angled her body so the guard would have his back to the doorway. The guard, though, started to look over his shoulder just as Clementine tried to sneak past.

"Ow!" Amal screamed, drawing the guard's attention back to her before he could spot Clementine. "The bees are biting me!"

The guard narrowed his eyes at Amal. "Don't you mean 'stinging'?" he said.

"Ow! Stinging!" Amal shouted. Then she collapsed on the floor.

Raining and Wilson ran in, and Clementine moved toward *Tiled Lunch Counter*.

"What happened to our friend?" Raining said, kneeling next to Amal on the floor.

"I don't know!" the guard said, taking off his hat and scratching his head. "She was shouting about bees, and then she just passed out!"

"She's allergic to bees!" Wilson hollered dramatically. "Why didn't you help her?"

"Help her?" the guard said. His eyes had gone wide and his face red. "I didn't even see any bees!"

With the guard totally distracted, Clementine climbed over the velvet rope and stepped right up to the painting. *Finally!* she thought.

But even face to face with the painting, Clementine was stumped. Ralph Goings was no ordinary painter, and this was no ordinary work of art. It was Photorealism at its best. Even finding Goings's brushstrokes was next to impossible in a painting that was meant to have the detail and smooth finish of an actual photograph.

"Hey!" roared the guard.

"Oh, no," Clementine whispered, bracing herself. Sure enough, she heard the big guard's heavy footsteps coming closer, and a moment later his hand was on her shoulder.

"I've had about enough of you!" the guard roared as Clementine turned around. "You and your friends — even the Bee Girl — out of this museum, this instant!"

"But you can't!" Clementine protested. "My mom —"

"I know who your mom is," the guard snapped back, shuffling her toward the door, "and I don't care."

When he'd reached the exit, the guard turned to Raining, Amal, and Wilson, who were all still crouched together in the middle of the gallery. Amal was no longer pretending to be passed out from bee stings.

"You three, too," the guard said, snapping his fingers. "Out of my gallery. Out of the museum."

The kids had no choice but to comply. The furious guard escorted them right through the big lobby to the front doors of the museum.

"I don't want to see you three here again. Got it?!" he shouted as they left.

"We got it!" Amal snapped. "Have a nice day!"

The guard huffed and turned his back on them to go resume his post in the special exhibit gallery.

"Now what?" Clementine said. She dropped to the sidewalk and leaned against the front of the museum, feeling dejected.

Amal held out her phone. "Call your mom," she said. "She'll let us back in, right?"

"Big deal if she does," Clementine said. "There's no way that big gorilla will let me get close again. And besides, it's not like it would do any good. I thought

I'd see something helpful once I got close to the painting, but I didn't see *any* brushstrokes at all!"

"Do you think your mom might be able to spot anything weird in the painting?" Wilson asked, sitting down next to her.

Clementine shook her head. "She thinks I've lost my marbles!" she said. "She definitely won't go check the painting, not after the stunt we just pulled."

"She won't have to go anywhere to check," Wilson said. "I have an idea."

Clementine lifted her chin. "What is it?" she asked.

"Do you have your bike here?" Wilson replied.

Clementine nodded.

Wilson held out his hand to help her up and said, "Give me a ride to my house."

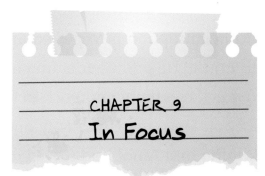

## CHAPTER 9
## In Focus

"She's pretty upset," Clementine said, covering the microphone of Amal's cell phone. On the other end, her mother shouted about how embarrassing it had been to get a report from the museum's head of security that her daughter had orchestrated a complicated diversion in order to sneak past a guard in the special exhibit.

"Will she let us back in?" Wilson asked as he fiddled with the long, black cylindrical contraption he'd picked up from his house. He and Clementine had made a quick trip there and back to the Art Museum. Since there was only one bike, Raining and Amal had stayed behind.

"Mom, I'm sorry," Clementine said. "I really am. I promise I won't go anywhere *near* the Goings painting again . . . yes . . . promise . . . thank you."

Clementine hung up and handed the phone to Amal. "She said we can come back in," she told her friends. "But we have to be on our best behavior. And we're still not allowed in the special exhibit gallery."

"That won't be a problem," Wilson said as he followed Clementine back into the Art Museum. "Not with what I have."

"Let's hope you're right," Clementine said, leading the way to the special exhibit gallery. They might not be allowed *inside*, but no one had said they couldn't observe from the hallway.

Once they'd reached the gallery, Wilson held the long, black cylinder — his digital telescope — to his eye.

"Can you see it?" Clementine said, bouncing on her toes.

"I just want to get it into focus for you . . . ," Wilson said. "There we go."

He handed it to Clementine, and she put it up to her right eye.

"I don't see anything," Clementine complained.

"That's because you've got the wrong eye open," Wilson said. He bit back his laughter, knowing Clementine wouldn't appreciate it.

"Oh, right," Clementine said. She closed her left eye and opened her right eye. "That's much better. I can see it now."

"Great," Raining said. "Does anything look weird?"

"Or suspicious?" Amal asked.

"Or forged?" Wilson added.

"Or photocopied?" Raining said.

Clementine stared and stared at the painting. She looked at the detail of the tiles themselves, and she looked at the men sitting at the counter — the wrinkles on their faces, the lines in their hair, and the stripes on their shirts — but she couldn't see anything weird at all.

"Oh, I just don't know!" Clementine said, exasperated. She lowered the telescope. "Ralph Goings was just too good at hiding his strokes. He was a pioneer of the genre!"

"Um," Wilson said, "so are you saying it's real?"

"I don't know!" Clementine said. "My mom might be able to tell, but she's not here, and she's so mad, you guys. I'm not going to ask her to —"

"She doesn't have to be here," Wilson said. "Give me that back." He took the telescope, held it up for a few moments, and then *click, click, click, click.*

"Did you just take pictures with that?" Amal asked.

Wilson nodded. "It can store images," he said. "Cool, huh?"

"Wow," Amal said. "You have to let me borrow that for stargazing."

"You got it," Wilson said. "Now let's bring these pictures to Dr. Wim."

## CHAPTER 10
## Gone for Good?

"Pictures of the Goings?" Dr. Wim said as she stood up from behind her desk. "Clementine Wim, I specifically told you *not* to go back to the special exhibit."

Clementine kept her eyes on her shoes. She was having a terrible day. Luckily, she had Amal with her.

"We didn't go in, Dr. Wim," Amal said quickly. "We were very careful to stay outside."

"But I had my digital telescope," Wilson said, holding it up. "I used that to take some detailed photos of the painting."

"Really?" Dr. Wim said, crossing her arms. "Let me see."

"I can't show you on this," Wilson said, "but I can bring them up on your computer display."

Dr. Wim looked at Clementine. "You're serious about this?" she said. "You really think something's not right?"

"I can't tell," Clementine said. "But I *know* I saw two people carrying *Tiled Lunch Counter* yesterday on the Big Lawn."

Dr. Wim took a deep, calming breath. "Fine," she said. "Wilson, can you bring up the images on the large displays in the conference room?"

"I don't see why not," Wilson said.

Dr. Wim nodded. "Then all of you, follow me. We'll get to the bottom of this."

The museum's main conference room had been recently renovated. What had once been a dreary, musty room with little more than a long table and a dozen chairs had been transformed into a state-of-the-art multimedia showpiece that the entire Capitol City Museums collection could be proud of.

In a few minutes, Wilson had hooked up his telescope. The four friends took a seat at the conference table, and Dr. Wim stood in front of the huge display at the front of the room. Wilson clicked through the images as Dr. Wim hummed thoughtfully.

"Let me see the first one again," Dr. Wim said. "Hmm . . . and the last one."

Finally, after looking at the images over and over, Dr. Wim sat at the head of the table. Her face was pale as she ran her hands through her hair, as red as her daughter's.

"What do you think?" Clementine asked anxiously, leaning forward in her chair.

Dr. Wim sighed. She gave Clementine a long, distant look. Finally she said, "It's not real. The brushstrokes are off, ever so slightly."

Clementine jumped to her feet. "You mean I was right?" she exclaimed.

"It appears so," Dr. Wim said. "But now what? We have to call the police, but the two people you saw yesterday morning are probably miles from here by now. Oh, this is so bad."

Clementine dropped back into her chair. "Oh, no," she said. "Then the real painting might be gone for good."

Dr. Wim knelt in front of her daughter's chair. "We should have listened to you yesterday," she said. "*I* should have listened to you. I'm sorry, Clementine."

"It was probably already too late when I finally told you about it anyway," Clementine said.

"Wait a minute," Amal said. "We're not just giving up, are we?"

"What can we even do?" Wilson asked. "Like Dr. Wim said, the crooks are probably long gone by now. And even if they were still in town, we have no way of finding them."

"Clementine saw them," Raining said.

Everyone looked at Clementine hopefully.

"So?" Clementine said. "What am I supposed to do, wander the city hunting for them?"

"What did they look like?" Amal asked.

Clementine thought about it for a moment and then said, "The man had a beard — big, bushy black beard. And he was so mean."

"And the other one?" Wilson said. "The woman?"

"She was nice," Clementine said. She let out a small laugh. "I actually gave her my phone number so she could call me if she saw you guys." She smacked herself in the forehead. "Of course my phone was in a lump of clay, so even if she —"

Suddenly Clementine sat up straight, her mouth and eyes wide. "I have to go home," she said.

"What?" Dr. Wim said, leaning back. "Right now?"

"Yes," said Clementine, standing up. "I'll be back as soon as I can." She headed for the door.

"I can drive you!" her mom called after her.

"It's faster to bike," Clementine called back over her shoulder. "I won't be long!"

## CHAPTER 11
## Cracking the Case

Clementine's old three-speed bike wasn't exactly the fastest or most aerodynamic bicycle on the road. It was heavy, and she was forced to sit upright like a girl out for a pleasant afternoon ride in the year 1890.

But today, none of that mattered. Clementine pedaled hard, sweating through her T-shirt. She pumped her legs as hard and fast as she could, and on the downhill parts, she loved the cooling breeze through her hair and on her neck and arms.

At her house, Clementine hopped onto the sidewalk and rode straight to the door of the shed. She jumped off the bike, letting it fall to the grass, and ran inside. Her abstract vase — its coat of ice-blue paint dry and shiny — sat where she'd left it in the middle of her worktable.

Clementine picked it up and held it in her hands like a thing of beauty. In her eyes, that's just what it was. "If I had my phone," she said to herself, "I'd take a picture of it."

But sadly, there was no time — or way — to do that. Clementine sighed and placed the vase carefully back on the table. Then she went to the wall of tools hung on pegs — screwdrivers, wrenches, pliers, hacksaws, and more — and grabbed a hammer and some plastic eye protection.

"Goodbye, perfect little accident," Clementine whispered to the vase as she slipped on the eye protection. "Oh, I hope this works."

With that, she raised the hammer and brought it down — swift, firm, and sure — on the sculpture, shattering it to blue and red dust.

As the cloud of debris cleared, Clementine coughed and pulled off her eyewear. She brushed aside the dust, and there it was — her phone. The battery was dead, but she had hope.

Clementine grabbed it, tugged its charger from the shed's outlet, and hopped back on her bike. She'd have to plug it in at the museum and pray for a miracle.

* * *

"I can't believe that thing still works," Amal said. "I dropped my phone into a bowl of macaroni and cheese once, and it never worked right again."

The four friends sat with Dr. Wim in her office. Clementine had her phone plugged in and was poking through screens to find missed calls.

"Good thing you didn't fire that piece," Dr. Wim pointed out, "or that phone would be molten."

Clementine's eyes went wide as she realized how right her mom was — and how close she'd come to losing the only clue she had. She'd planned on firing it to shine the glaze that very evening.

"Okay," Clementine said, scrolling through the incoming calls. "I missed a call yesterday morning. There's a message."

Clementine tapped the play button, and noise crackled through the speaker. The voices were muffled, as if the people on the other end were far away — or as if they didn't know the phone was on.

"What were you thinking, letting that kid put her phone number in my phone?" a man's angry voice said. "If you call her we'll be caught for sure! Use your head, Polly!"

"Oh, lighten up, Curt!" a woman's voice replied. "I'm not actually going to call her! How stupid do you think I am? She just looked so lost; I couldn't resist giving her a little hope. I'll delete her number as soon as we get the painting in your truck."

With that the voices trailed off. The phone continued recording, picking up the sounds of footsteps, as well as the noises of the Dino Festival — presumably as the couple made their way through the crowd.

Dr. Wim pulled her reading glasses down from her head and shook her head in astonishment. "They must have butt-dialed you. What's the number that left that message?" she asked. She wrote it down as Clementine read it aloud. "Time to call the police in on this one."

## CHAPTER 12
## Nearly Perfect

When the police arrived at the
museum thirty minutes later, they came
bearing an arrest warrant. The four
friends and Dr. Wim met the police
detective and two uniformed officers in
the front lobby.

"Who's that warrant for?" Dr. Wim asked.

"Is there an employee at this museum named Curtis Clump?" the detective asked her.

Dr. Wim shook her head no. "I've never heard that name before," she said. "But that doesn't necessarily mean he doesn't work here. He could work in maintenance . . . or security. I don't know either of those teams very well."

The detective nodded to the officers, and they headed toward the information desk. After a moment, one of them turned back to the detective.

"Our perp's in the special exhibit gallery!" he called.

"Pick him up," the detective said. Then she turned to Dr. Wim. "We'll have to seize the copy, too. It's evidence."

"Of course," Dr. Wim said. "I just wish we could hang the original in its place."

"We'll find it," the detective assured her. "Excuse me." She hurried after her officers.

"What did they mean?" Clementine asked. "The perp's in the special exhibit gallery? How would they know that?"

"He must work here, like the detective said," Raining pointed out.

Amal's jaw dropped. "You don't think . . . ," she said slowly. "It can't be *him*."

"Who?" Clementine asked, still confused, but then suddenly it struck her. The perp didn't have the big black beard, but he *had* looked familiar — and he was obviously incredibly mean. "The security guard! No wonder he wouldn't let me near *Tiled Lunch Counter*! He knew it was a fake!"

The four friends and Dr. Wim ran to the Photorealism gallery just in time to see the detective handcuffing Curt Clump. At the same time, the two officers pulled the *Tiled Lunch Counter* off the wall.

"This is a copy?" one of the officers said. "Of what, a photograph?"

"I don't know what you're talking about!" Curt shouted.

"Do you deny calling this girl's cell phone at," the detective said, checking her notes, "10:27 yesterday morning?"

"Yes!" Curt said. "I never called anyone yesterday morning!"

"How can you be so sure?" the detective asked.

"Because my girlfriend has had my phone since two nights ago," Curt said. "Maybe she called the little weirdo. I sure didn't!"

"And your girlfriend's name is . . . ?" the detective said.

Curt's face went red. "Polly Plum," he said.

The detective wrote down the name in her notebook. Then she turned and nodded at her officers. The two men took Curt by the arm and led him out of the gallery.

"They'll put him in the car," the detective told Dr. Wim and the kids. "Meanwhile, I'll get to work tracking down Plum. I have a feeling we'll have that painting back where it belongs in no time."

"Thank you, Detective," Dr. Wim said gratefully.

The detective turned to Clementine. "The first thing I'd like to try is for you to call Polly from your phone," she instructed. "It's a long shot, but maybe your number is still saved in there, and she'll answer without thinking about it. Do you mind?"

Clementine shrugged. "Why not," she said. She tapped her phone, brought up the missed calls again, and tapped *call back*.

After a moment, it rang. In fact, every single person in the room heard it ring — from around the corner.

The detective's eyebrows went up. "She's here," she said.

"Hello?" came a voice through the phone.

"Um . . . hi," Clementine said, stalling a bit. "This is Clementine — the girl from the Big Lawn yesterday? Is this Polly?"

"Yes, it is," Polly answered. "Did you ever manage to find your — hey, wait a minute. I never told you my name. How did you —"

But by then, the detective had found Polly in the next gallery over. She was standing in front of a painting of a case full of silver cups, saucers, and pitchers on glass shelves. Clementine put away her phone and strode up behind the woman.

Polly held up her hands. "I'm not going to run or anything," she said to the detective, who had pulled out her handcuffs. "I just wanted everyone to see my Goings copy."

"It's very good," Clementine admitted a little reluctantly.

"Thank you," Polly said. "I'm an art student. I copied it for one of my classes, and . . . well, I thought if I fooled the best eyes in the world, maybe I'd have a shot at becoming one of the greats in Photorealism."

"You do have a shot," Dr. Wim said as she walked up. "Mind you, you didn't quite fool me, not when I got a closer look. But you obviously have a tremendous amount of talent."

"You really mean it?" Polly asked.

Dr. Wim nodded and smiled, but in the next moment the detective stepped between them. She slipped the cuffs onto Polly's wrists.

"And the best part is," the detective said, "you'll have plenty of time to practice in your cell."

Polly's face fell, but after a moment she shrugged. "Actually, that's a good point," she said.

"Where is the original?" Dr. Wim asked. "That's all I'm really concerned about."

"In my apartment downtown," Polly said. "You know, I never would have tried this swap if Curt hadn't suggested it. He just wanted to sell the Goings painting so he could quit this job and follow his dream."

"What's his dream?" said Amal.

"High-concept balloon animals," Polly said.

Everyone was speechless for a moment. Finally, the detective coughed. "Come along to the car now," she said. "Curt is waiting for you to head off to jail."

Polly nodded and let the detective drag her along. But after a few steps, she stopped and looked at Clementine. "You know," she said, "no good deed goes unpunished."

"What do you mean?" Clementine asked.

"If I hadn't stopped to take your number," Polly continued, "we might have gotten away with it."

"All right, that's enough. Come on," the detective said. Polly followed her out of the gallery.

Dr. Wim put an arm around Clementine. "I'm proud of you," she told her daughter.

"Why?" Clementine asked, shaking her head. "It was just dumb luck that we found them."

"But you knew something was wrong," Dr. Wim said, "even when your best friends didn't believe you. Even when *I* didn't believe you."

"Thanks, Mom," Clementine said, blushing. "I really thought I was losing my mind."

"Hey," Amal said, giving the taller girl a little shove, "no one said you *haven't* lost it."

"Ha ha," Clementine said dryly. "Very funny."

"Tell us about this one, Clem," Wilson said, taking her hand, and pulling her over to the painting Polly had been studying.

"Oh!" Clementine said, gazing up at the startling realism of the silver pieces.

"This one is by Don Eddy, and it's called *Silverware*, from 1976. They really seem to shine, don't they?"

"They sure do, Clementine," Raining said. "They sure do."

Steve B.

## About the Author

Steve Brezenoff is the author of more than fifty middle-grade chapter books, including the Field Trip Mysteries series, the Ravens Pass series of thrillers, and the Return to Titanic series. In his spare time, he enjoys video games, cycling, and cooking. Steve lives in Minneapolis with his wife, Beth, and their son and daughter.

Lisa W.

## About the Illustrator

Lisa K. Weber is an illustrator currently living in Oakland, California. She graduated from Parsons School of Design in 2000 and then began freelancing. Since then, she has completed many print, animation, and design projects, including graphic novelizations of classic literature, character and background designs for children's cartoons, and textiles for dog clothing.

# GLOSSARY

**abstract** (ab-STRAKT) — in art, expressing ideas and emotions by using elements such as colors and lines without attempting to create a realistic picture

**aerodynamic** (air-oh-dahy-NAM-ik) — the qualities of an object that affect how easily it is able to move through the air

**counterfeit** (KOUN-ter-fit) — made to look like an exact copy of something in order to trick people

**debris** (duh-BREE) — the pieces that are left after something has been destroyed

**dreary** (DREER-ee) — having nothing likely to provide cheer, comfort, or interest

**evidence** (EV-uh-duhnss) — information and facts that help prove something or make you believe something is true

**exhibit** (eg-ZIB-it) — a public display of works of art, historical objects, etc.

**gallery** (GAL-uh-ree) — a room or building in which people look at paintings, sculptures, etc.

**Photorealism** (foh-toh-REE-uh-liz-uhm) — a style of painting characterized by extremely meticulous depiction of detail; works of art so real they look like photographs

**seize** (SEEZ) — to use legal or official power to take something

# DISCUSSION QUESTIONS

**1.** Do you think Amal was right to be irritated with Clementine for the way she acted in the beginning of this story? Talk about why or why not.

**2.** Clementine and her friends ultimately solved the case, even though there weren't many suspects. Talk about how you would have tackled this mystery. Did you suspect anyone else in the course of reading this story?

**3.** Art is Clementine's favorite hobby, but her friends all have their own interests and hobbies. Talk about one of your own hobbies. What do you like about it? What makes it so interesting?

# WRITING PROMPTS

**1.** Ralph Goings's *Tiled Lunch Counter* is a famous painting and great example of Photorealism. Do some research on the Photorealism movement and write a paragraph about what you learn.

**2.** There are four major museums in the Capitol City network — the Natural History Museum, the Air and Space Museum, the Art Museum, and the American History Museum. Write a paragraph about which museum you would be most interested in and why.

**3.** Clementine stuck to her convictions, even when no one believed her. Write a paragraph about a time you had to stick up for yourself, even in the face of disbelief, or write about what you would have done in Clementine's position.

# MORE ABOUT PHOTOREALISM

There are many different types and styles of art, sometimes called genres. Photorealism, which can also be referred to as "Hyper-Realism," "Super-Realism," or "New Realism," is one such genre. This style of art involves an artist studying a photograph and then attempting to reproduce the image as realistically as possible using his or her chosen medium — be it painting, drawing, or another graphic medium. Many times the images being reproduced involve near-microscopic detail and focus on surface, such as glass, reflections, or the effects of light.

Photorealism, which first began in the late 1960s in California and New York, was given its name by art dealer and gallery owner Louis K. Meisel in 1969. Meisel published a formal five-point definition of the movement, which read:

1. The photorealist uses the camera and photograph to gather information.

2. The photorealist uses a mechanical or semi-mechanical means to transfer the information to the canvas.

3. The photorealist must have the technical ability to make the finished work appear photographic.

4. The artist must have exhibited work as a photorealist by 1972 to be considered one of the central photorealists.

5. The artist must have devoted at least five years to the development and exhibition of photorealist work.

Despite that strict definition, many artists practicing Photorealism didn't follow those exact guidelines. Some of the early American pioneers of the Photorealism movement included Ralph Goings, Chuck Close, Malcolm Morley, Richard Estes, Audrey Flack, Robert Bechtle, Denis Peterson, and Don Eddy. While Photorealism was a largely American movement, there were supporters in Europe as well, particularly in England and France, including English painter John Salt and Swiss painter Franz Gertsch.

Ready for more
MYSTERY?

# MUSEUM MYSTERIES

Check out another Capitol City sleuths' adventure and help them solve crime in some of the city's most important museums!

STEVE BREZENOFF

MUSEUM MYSTERIES

The Case of the
Stolen Space Suit

When the space suit of famous astronaut Sally Ride is stolen from a traveling exhibit, there's no shortage of suspects in Capitol City. Thankfully, Amal Farah, daughter of the Air and Space Museum's head archivist, and her friends are on the case. But they're running out of time, and clues are hard to come by. Can they solve the mystery of the space case before the one-of-a-kind artifact is lost for good?